The Three Little Pigs

Once upon a time, there lived three little pigs: Wilbur, Barnaby, and Hamlet. One day, when they were all grown up, they decided to leave home and build their very own houses.

Before they left, their mother told them to always remember two things: to always work hard, no matter what, and to never, ever let a stranger into their home—especially not the Big Bad Wolf!

Each brother had a different idea of the perfect house, so they each decided to build their own home. They found a perfect clearing in the forest where they could all live side by side. Then, they spent the rest of the afternoon gathering the items they needed.

Barnaby was the laziest brother. He wasn't interested in working very hard, and just wanted to build his home the quickest and easiest way. He gathered straw from a nearby field and hastily put his house together in only one day!

Hamlet was a bit more practical. He knew that straw was very weak, so instead he gathered all the sticks he could find in the forest and tied them together. His home was slightly sturdier than Barnaby's, and took him two days to build.

Wilbur, the eldest brother, was the most dedicated to building his home. He gathered bricks and mortar and built walls and a chimney. He spent a full week building his house. His brothers teased him for working so hard.

"What a waste of time!" they chided. "You could have finished a long time ago!"

But Wilbur liked his new home and knew it was the sturdiest one.

When all three pigs were done building, they retreated to their homes. While Barnaby and Hamlet lazed around in the sunshine, Wilbur continued to work hard. He made himself some furniture, and gathered food and supplies.

Meanwhile, the three little pigs had no idea that the Big Bad Wolf was spying on them. It was the very same wolf that their mother had warned them about! He wanted to eat the pigs for dinner.

"I'll trick those silly pigs into letting me in… and then I'll eat them up!" he said as he licked his chops.

The next morning, Barnaby heard a knock at his door. When he peered through the peephole, he saw the Big Bad Wolf that his mother had warned him about.

“I’m not letting you in, Mr. Wolf! Not by the hair on my chinny-chin-chin,” said the little pig sternly.

The wolf had a very bad temper, and didn't like to be refused.

"Then I'll huff, and I'll puff, and I'll blow your house down!" cried the angry wolf.

And with one big breath, Barnaby's straw home collapsed.

The frightened pig scurried next door to his brother Hamlet's stick house.

"The Big Bad Wolf just blew my house down!" Barnaby sobbed. "And he's chasing me!"

Hamlet hurried to make sure the door was locked securely.

Just then, there was a rap on Hamlet's door.

"Little pigs, little pigs, let me come in!" growled the wolf.

"No! Not by the hair on our chinny-chin-chins!" shrieked the pigs.

"Then I'll huff, and I'll puff, and I'll blow your house down!" said the wolf.

And that's just what he did!

The two brothers were scared. They ran to Wilbur's brick home as fast as they could.

“Help!” they shouted. “The Big Bad Wolf is coming!”

They told Wilbur that the wolf had blown both their houses down. Then, they heard a knock on the door.

By the time he reached Wilbur's house, the wolf was very hungry.

"I'll huff, and I'll puff, and I'll blow your house down!" the wolf yelled.

The wolf huffed and he puffed. Then he huffed and he puffed some more. But the brick house didn't budge!

Furious, the wolf searched for another way into the house. He spotted the chimney up on the roof and had an idea! He decided to catch the pigs by surprise and drop in through the fireplace. He climbed the brick wall and made his way onto the roof.

All the while, Wilbur could hear the wolf shuffling around on the rooftop.

"He's trying to make his way in through the chimney!" Wilbur predicted. "Don't worry, I have a plan."

Wilbur lit a fire in the hearth. Soon, a great fire was blazing in the fireplace.

"What good will a fire do at a time like this?" Barnaby asked.

Just then, the wolf fell down the chimney and right into the fire!

“That’s what you get for trying to sneak in through the chimney!” said Wilbur.

The wolf howled in pain and ran out the front door. The three little pigs squealed with delight and locked the door behind him.

The wolf ran deep into the forest, his tail ablaze, and jumped in the lake. He may have been able to trick Hamlet and Barnaby, but if he thought he could outsmart clever Wilbur, he was sorely mistaken!

Although they had laughed at their brother's brick house, Hamlet and Barnaby now understood how wise he was.

"We're sorry we teased you about your brick house," Hamlet apologized.

"Will you help us build our own brick houses?" asked Barnaby.

"I'll help you, as long as you promise to work hard," said Wilbur.

"Of course!" his brothers replied.

From that day forward, the three little pigs worked hard at everything they did, and they never heard from the Big Bad Wolf again. They all lived happily ever after in their sturdy brick homes!